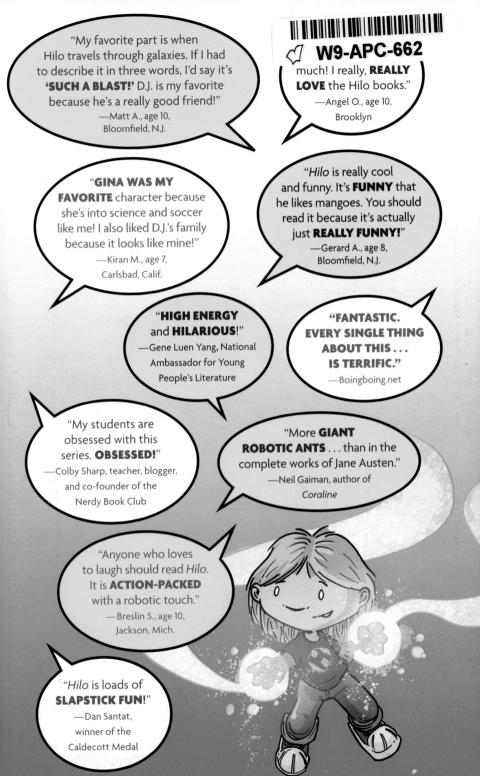

"My favorite part is when Hilo travels through galaxies. If I had to describe it in three words, I'd say it's **'SUCH A BLAST!'** D.J. is my favorite because he's a really good friend!"
—Matt A., age 10, Bloomfield, N.J.

much! I really, **REALLY LOVE** the Hilo books."
—Angel O., age 10, Brooklyn

"**GINA WAS MY FAVORITE** character because she's into science and soccer like me! I also liked D.J.'s family because it looks like mine!"
—Kiran M., age 7, Carlsbad, Calif.

"*Hilo* is really cool and funny. It's **FUNNY** that he likes mangoes. You should read it because it's actually just **REALLY FUNNY!**"
—Gerard A., age 8, Bloomfield, N.J.

"**HIGH ENERGY** and **HILARIOUS**!"
—Gene Luen Yang, National Ambassador for Young People's Literature

"FANTASTIC. EVERY SINGLE THING ABOUT THIS . . . IS TERRIFIC."
—Boingboing.net

"My students are obsessed with this series. **OBSESSED!**"
—Colby Sharp, teacher, blogger, and co-founder of the Nerdy Book Club

"More **GIANT ROBOTIC ANTS** . . . than in the complete works of Jane Austen."
—Neil Gaiman, author of *Coraline*

"Anyone who loves to laugh should read *Hilo*. It is **ACTION-PACKED** with a robotic touch."
—Breslin S., age 10, Jackson, Mich.

"*Hilo* is loads of **SLAPSTICK FUN**!"
—Dan Santat, winner of the Caldecott Medal

READ ALL THE HILO BOOKS!
HILO #1 THE BOY WHO CRASHED TO EARTH
HILO #2 SAVING THE WHOLE WIDE WORLD
HILO #3 THE GREAT BIG BOOM
HILO #4 WAKING THE MONSTERS
HILO #5 THEN EVERYTHING WENT WRONG
HILO #6 ALL THE PIECES FIT
HILO #7 GINA: THE GIRL WHO BROKE THE WORLD

HILO Book 7: Gina—The Girl Who Broke the World

BY JUDD WINICK

COLOR BY
MAARTA LAIHO

RANDOM HOUSE NEW YORK

With grateful thanks to our authenticity reader, Shasta Clinch, for her thoughtful feedback, insights, and perspective. This book is better because of it.

Visit us on the Web! rhcbooks.com

Educators and librarians, for a variety of teaching tools, visit us at RHTeachersLibrarians.com

Library of Congress Cataloging-in-Publication Data
Names: Winick, Judd, author. | Laiho, Maarta, colorist.
Title: Hilo. Book 7, Gina, the girl who broke the world / by Judd Winick; color by Maarta Laiho.
Other titles: Gina, the girl who broke the world
Description: First edition. | New York: Random House Children's Books, [2021]
Summary: "With the help of her friends DJ and Hilo, Gina protects magical beings who've just appeared on Earth from the creatures who are after them." —Provided by publisher.
Identifiers: LCCN 2020025250 | ISBN 978-0-525-64409-5 (hardcover)
ISBN 978-0-525-64410-1 (library binding) | ISBN 978-0-525-64411-8 (ebook)
Subjects: LCSH: Graphic novels. | CYAC: Graphic novels. | Magic—Fiction. | Imaginary creatures—Fiction. | Robots—Fiction. | Extraterrestrial beings—Fiction. | Science fiction.
Classification: LCC PZ7.7.W57 Ho 2021 | DDC 741.5/973—dc23

Book design by Bob Bianchini

MANUFACTURED IN CHINA

10 9 8 7 6 5 4 3 2 1

First Edition

For
David

CHAPTER

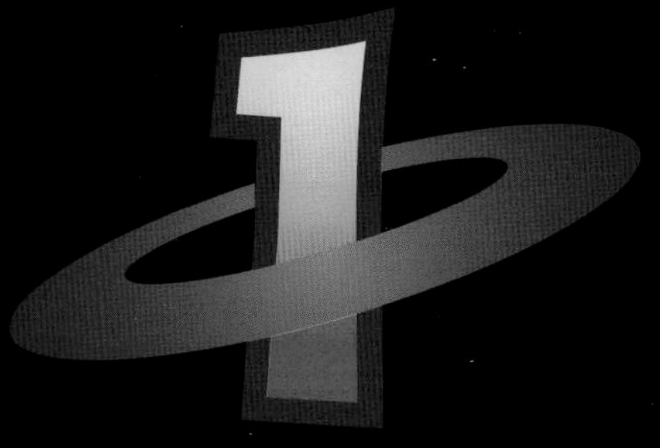

I GOT THIS

MY NAME IS **REGINA LEE COOPER.**

YOU OKAY?!

SORT OF!

BUT EVERYONE CALLS ME **GINA.**

AND I'M HAVING A WEIRD DAY.

YOU FIND HIM?!

I FOUND HIM!

BUT **A LOT** OF MY DAYS ARE WEIRD.
TZOT

UH-OH.

TZOT

GINA?

AAAAAAAA
GINA?
AAAA-
AAAAH
BOOMP
ARE YOU OKAY?!
AAAAAAAAH!

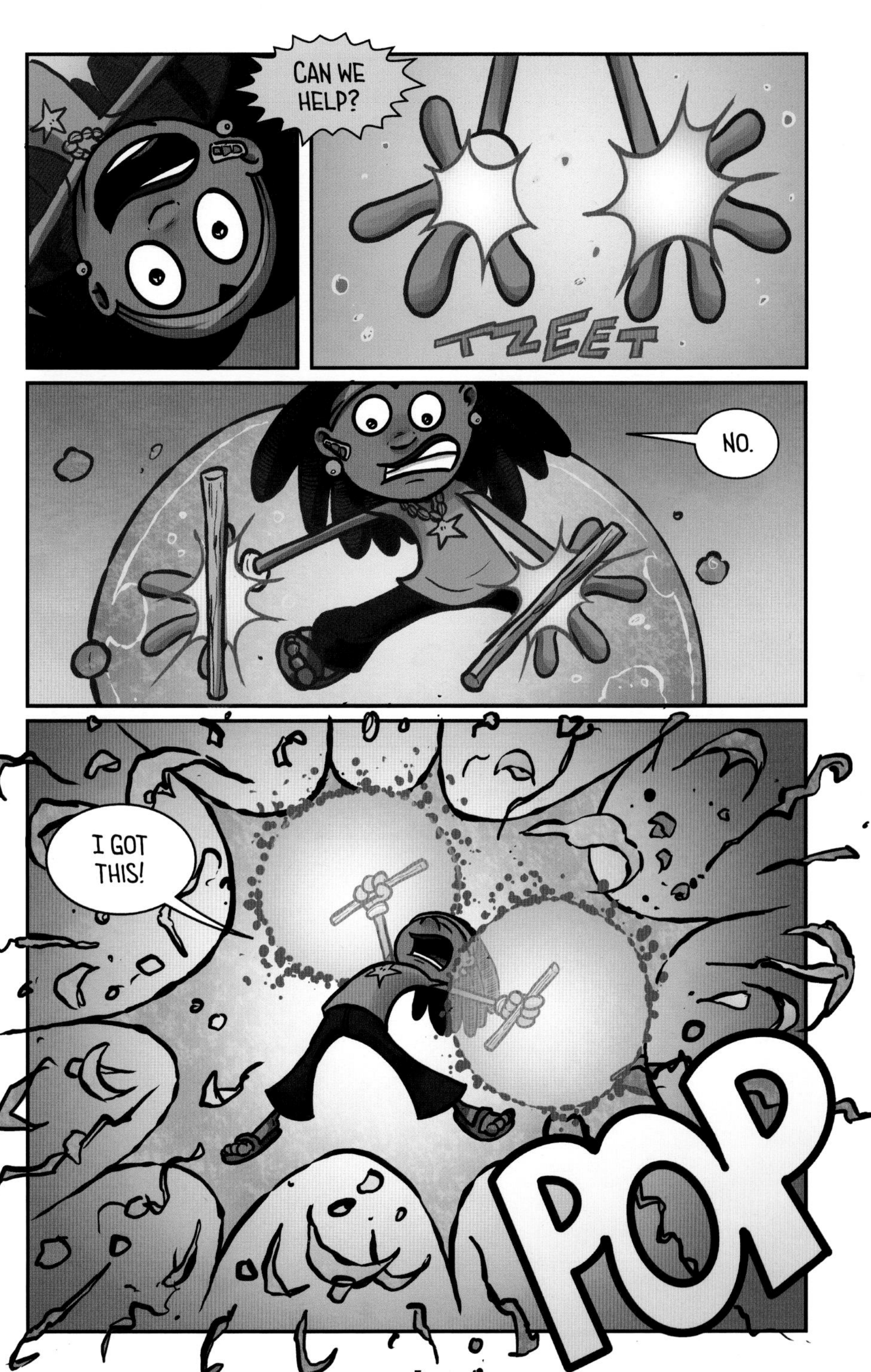
CAN WE HELP?
TZEET
NO.
I GOT THIS!
POP

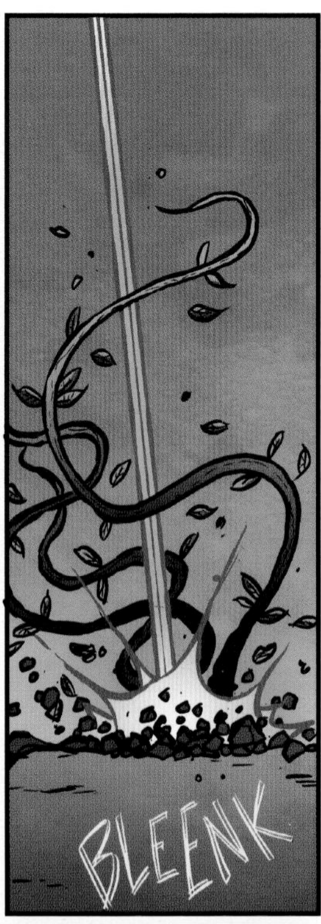

CROOOONK

AAAAAAAAA
YOU DON'T **SOUND** OKAY!!
I'LL BE FIIIIIIIIIIIIIIIIIIIIIIIIIIIIINE!
AAAAAAAA--
???

AAAAAAAAA

AAAAAAAAAAA
GINA?!

AAAA--

?

DOOMP

SKIIIIIIIIIIIIIIIIIIIID

BONK

NOT COOL! **ALL** KINDS OF **NOT COOL!**

AND I RIPPED THESE JEANS! I **LIKE** THESE JEANS!
GINA?!
YOU OKAY?!

BUT I'M **PREEEEETTY** SURE SOMETHING'S **ABOUT** TO HAPPEN.

FOUR DAYS EARLIER

THESE ARE MY FOUR BEST FRIENDS.

D.J. WHO I'VE KNOWN SINCE I WAS LITTLE.

POLLY. WHO'S FROM ANOTHER PLANET. AND **YES,** IS A CAT. WHO CAN TALK. AND DO MAGIC.

AND THERE'S **HILO** AND **IZZY.** WHO ARE **ALSO** FROM ANOTHER PLANET. JUST A DIFFERENT ONE FROM POLLY.

HILO AND IZZY ARE BOTH **ROBOTS.** HILO WAS SUPERSTRONG, COULD FLY, SHOOT LASERS FROM HIS HANDS, AND DO OTHER STUFF.

IZZY COULD MAKE ANYTHING JUST BY THINKING ABOUT IT.
IT'S AN **AARDVARK** WHO BURPS COTTON CANDY.
BORB
OUTSTANDING.
DELICIOUS.
PASS.

THEY WERE MADE BY THIS EVIL ROBOT NAMED **RAZORWARK.** HE WANTED TO DESTROY ALL THE PEOPLE ON THEIR PLANET.

THEY FOUGHT HIM.
IZZY GAVE ALL HER ENERGY TO HILO SO HE COULD STOP HIM.

AND HE DID. HILO WON. HE SAVED THE PEOPLE ON HIS PLANET.
HE SHOWED RAZORWARK HOW TO BE GOOD.
AND THEN...
RAZORWARK WAS GONE.

BUT SO WAS IZZY.

IT'S BEEN HARD.
WE MISS IZZY.

SOMETIMES I WAKE UP... AND I'VE FORGOTTEN SHE'S GONE.

THEN...I REMEMBER.

SOMETIMES I SEE HILO...
AND I KNOW HE'S THINKING ABOUT HER TOO.
BUT HE HIDES IT.

HE KEEPS BUSY. BECAUSE HERE'S THE AMAZING THING: AFTER THE WHOLE BATTLE WITH RAZORWARK...HE BECAME **HUMAN.**
HEY!
AND HE **LOVES** IT.

HOLY MACKEREL! I JUST WENT TO THE **BATHROOM!**
I KNOW.

POOPING IS **OUTSTANDING!**

I'M GONNA GO AGAIN!
IT DOESN'T WORK LIKE THAT!

HILO LIVES WITH D.J.
BEEP
HOLD STILL FOR THE TIMER.

CLICK
HE'S JOINED THE **LIM** FAMILY.

OKAY. NOW A **"HILO"** PICTURE.
OF COURSE.

BUT IT MIGHT BE **MORE** LIKE THE LIM FAMILY HAS JOINED **HILO.**

HILO IS JUST GETTING USED TO ALL HIS NEW HUMAN SENSES.
MY FACE HURTS!
THAT'S BECAUSE THE CURRY IS SPICY.
DRINK THE MILK.

WHO WANTS MORE?

D.J.'S **MOM** AND SISTER **LISA** ARE THE ONLY ONES WHO KNOW THE TRUTH ABOUT WHAT HILO USED TO BE.

SMELL THIS! IT'S **HORRIBLE.**
YOU JUST NEED TO SHOWER.

MY RIGHT PIT IS EVEN **WORSE.**
THEY'RE COOL.

HIS NEW LIFE IS TAKING A **LITTLE** WORK.
WHUMP
CAFF
YOU FORGOT THAT YOU CAN'T FLY AGAIN.
I FORGOT THAT I CAN'T FLY AGAIN!
IT'S DIFFERENT FOR HIM NOW.

IT'S DIFFERENT FOR ME TOO.
WHEN WE VISITED **POLLY'S** WORLD, I LEARNED TO DO A LITTLE **MAGIC.**
AND WHEN WE GOT HOME, I COULD DO EVEN **MORE.**
AT FIRST IT SEEMED FUN.
BUT NOW...
IT'S DIFFERENT.

IT'S DIFFERENT IN A LOT OF WAYS.

TEEK.

HILO HAS CHANGED.

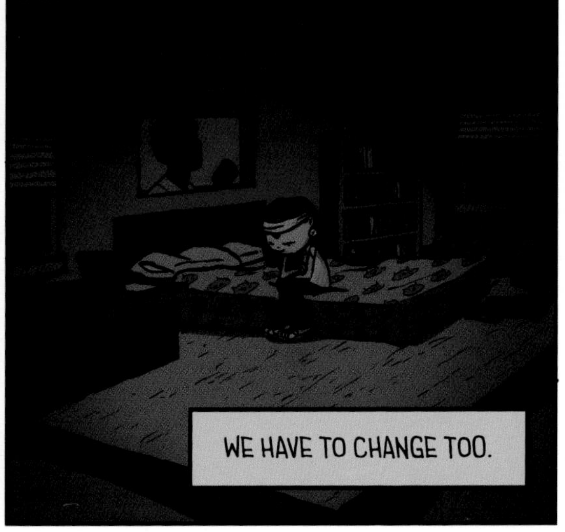
WE HAVE TO CHANGE TOO.

SCHOOL FIELD TRIP.
CASTRO MOON MUSEUM OF NATURAL HISTORY

LOOK AT THAT BAD BOY!

DID YOU KNOW THAT THE BLUE WHALE--BALAENOPTERA MUSCULUS--CAN WEIGH UP TO 210 TONS! ITS LIVER CAN WEIGH MORE THAN 2,500 POUNDS!

THAT'S 10 PERCENT OF THE WEIGHT OF THE ENTIRE WHALE! THAT'S A LOT OF LIVER.

YOU KNOW WHAT WOULD MAKE THIS WHALE **BETTER?**
IF IT WAS ALIVE AND COULD FLY.

IF IT WAS **ALIVE** AND COULD **FLY!**

YEAH! CUZ I'D **LOVE** TO RIDE A FLYING WHALE AGAIN LIKE WE DID ON **POLLY'S** PLANET.

AND WHEN I SAY **THAT**--I AM JUST KIDDING! A **JOKE!** I HAVE **NEVER** RIDDEN A FLYING WHALE, AND I DON'T KNOW ANY **TALKING CATS** FROM **MAGICAL PLANETS!**

I'M GETTING **SO** GOOD AT COVERING UP WHEN I ACCIDENTALLY MENTION THE STUFF WE'VE DONE.

WINK

OH! THEY'RE FEEDING THE PENGUINS! OUTSTANDING!
HE IS GETTING A LITTLE BETTER AT FITTING IN. DON'T YOU THINK?
WELL...

WHAT'S KICKIN', CHICKENS?!
FISH

I AM AWARE THAT YOU ARE PENGUINS! BUT I LIKE ASKING "WHAT'S KICKIN', CHICKENS?!"
FISH

WHAT?
FISH

PENGUINS DIG HILO. I THOUGHT WEIRD STUFF LIKE THAT WOULD STOP NOW THAT HE'S HUMAN.
ME TOO. BUT I THINK PEOPLE **LIKE** HOW WEIRD HE IS.

GERTIE LIKES HIM.
YEAH.
ERIC TOO.
YEAH?
YEAH.

WOOOOOOOOOOO OO OOOOOOO

OOOOOOOOOOO

WHOA. I WONDER WHAT'S HAPPENING.
WOOOOO

SOMEONE POSTED IT. THERE'S A HUGE **FIRE** AT THE LEHNER BUILDING.

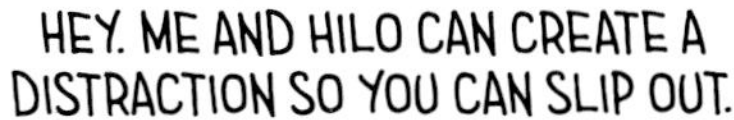
HEY. ME AND HILO CAN CREATE A DISTRACTION SO YOU CAN SLIP OUT.

WHAT?

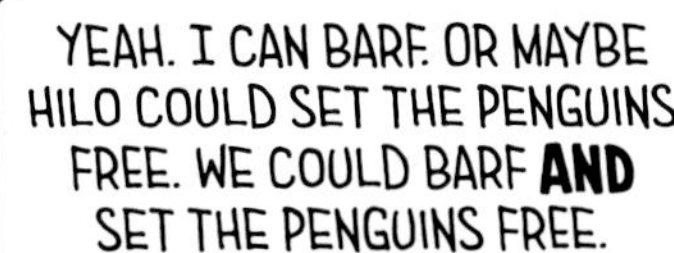
YEAH. I CAN BARF. OR MAYBE HILO COULD SET THE PENGUINS FREE. WE COULD BARF **AND** SET THE PENGUINS FREE.

NO, I MEAN, **WHY** WOULD I NEED TO SLIP OUT?

WELL. TO HELP OUT WITH THE FIRE.

YOU COULD DO SOME OF YOUR MAGIC.

Y'KNOW. **SUPERHERO** STUFF.

NO. THE FIREFIGHTERS WILL HANDLE IT.

I **KNOW,** BUT I JUST THOUGHT--

AND THE POLICE. **THEY** CAN HANDLE IT TOO.

THEY DON'T NEED ME.

WHO WANTS MANGO?
I DO.
ME TOO.
OKAY. I ONLY HAVE **FIVE** SO WE'LL HAVE TO SHARE.

D.J.'S HOUSE.

FIRE
DOWNTOWN

THAT LOOKS PRETTY SCARY.
AAH!

I DIDN'T HEAR YOU. HOW DO YOU MOVE SO **QUIETLY?**
I DON'T KNOW. MANGO?
NO, THANKS.

THAT FIRE WAS PRETTY TERRIBLE. LUCKILY NO ONE WAS HURT.
YEAH.

IT MADE GINA SUPER NERVOUS.
IT DID?

OH, YEAH. THIS IS EXCELLENT MANGO.
HOW DO YOU KNOW SHE WAS NERVOUS? I--

DUDES-- DINNER!
OUTSTANDING! VEGGIE STIR FRY! SPICY KIND!

I GOT MY OWN MILK!
MILK

WHERE DOES HE STOCKPILE MANGOES AND MILK?!
MOM BOUGHT HIM A MINI FRIDGE.

I CAN'T GET A PHONE, AND HE GETS A MINI FRIDGE?

NEWSNEWS
FIRE DOWNTOWN

CHAPTER
3

SEE THAT?

REALLY?
YES.
Vanderbilt Elementary School
YOU WANT TO TAKE BALLET?
YEP. I LIKE THE TIGHTS. LIKE **SPIDER-MAN.**
IT'S DIFFERENT FROM SPIDER-MAN.

I'M **HUMAN** NOW, AND I WANNA DO **NEW** THINGS. BALLET. TIGHTS. BANJO. LEARN TO MAKE GUACAMOLE. NEW STUFF.

MAYBE SOME KNITTING!

OR RAISING CHINCHILLAS!

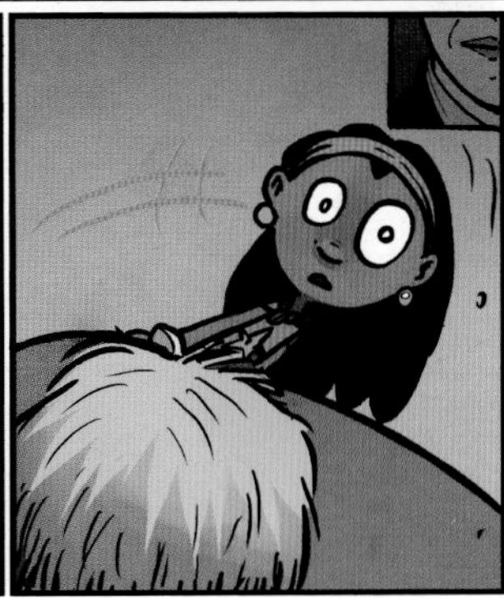

CRUD AND SCRAMBLED EGGS.

WHAT?

WHAT? **THAT!**

WHAT?
THAT TREE?

YOU DON'T SEE...?

NEVER MIND.

I NEED TO BARF AND SET SOME PENGUINS FREE.
WHAT?
NOTHING!

MR. TOLLIVER! MAY I PLEASE GO TO THE NURSE?

SURE. WHAT'S WRO--
TUESDAY

MY STOMACH.
MY HEAD.
YEAH.
MY STOMACH **AND** MY HEAD.
I--

HEEEM

THANKS!!

HEY THERE, MADAM!

OR SIR! PERSON! OR MAYBE NONE OF THOSE! **HEY!**

I'M **GINA!** WHO ARE YOU?

MY NAME AND MY TASK ARE NONE OF **YOUR** CONCERN.

GOT IT! BUT MAYBE I CAN HELP! I **THINK** I'M THE **ONLY** ONE WHO CAN SEE YOU, SO I FIGURE THAT YOU MUST BE **MAGICAL.** BECAUSE I, WELL, I CAN DO SOME MAGIC AND STUFF. AND--

CREEEOK
WHOA!

HEY! WHATCHA DOING THERE?! I WOULD ASK THAT YOU STOP. BECAUSE-- WELL, THAT LOOKS **PRETTY** UNUSUAL AND--

WOW-- SMELLS LIKE A POSSUM'S BUTT.

TROOOM

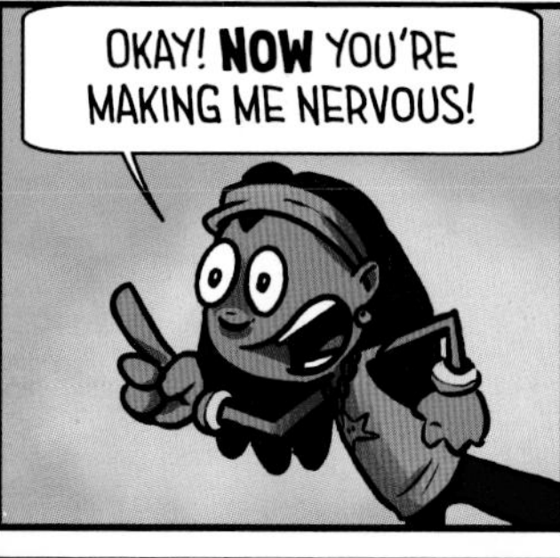
OKAY! **NOW** YOU'RE MAKING ME NERVOUS!

GINA, WHO ARE YOU TALKING TO?

WHAT ARE YOU DOING OUT HERE?
YOU WERE PRETENDING TO BE SICK. HILO SAID YOU WERE SUPER NERVOUS.
I **DID.**

SO WE PRETENDED TO BE SICK TOO.
WE BARFED.

AND I GOT A NOSE-BLEED!
YOU GUYS ARE **REALLY** GOOD AT THAT NOW.
I KNOW, RIGHT?

WHO ARE YOU TALKING TO?
NO ONE!

BOOM

OH, I MEAN--I DON'T KNOW! THERE'S A CREATURE-PERSON-THING--AND I THINK I'M THE ONLY ONE WHO CAN SEE HIM!

CONCENTRATE. THINK ABOUT MAKING HIM REVEAL HIMSELF.

WHAT?

YOU CAN DO MAGIC. THIS IS MAGIC. IT'S YOUR POWER. WHEN I HAD THE POWERS, I WOULD CONCENTRATE ON THE THING I WANTED TO HAPPEN.

CONCENTRATE.
THAT'S YOUR POWER.

TINK
OOOOOM

AAAH!
OUTSTANDING.

YOU CAN SEE HIM NOW?
YEAH!
WHAT'S KICKIN', CHICKEN?!

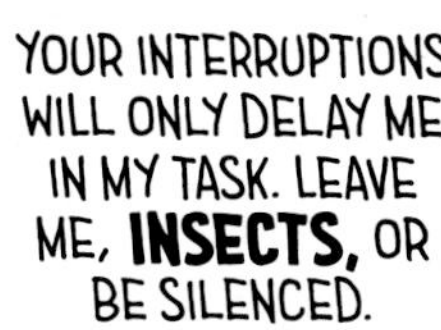
YOUR INTERRUPTIONS WILL ONLY DELAY ME IN MY TASK. LEAVE ME, **INSECTS,** OR BE SILENCED.

KIND OF RUDE.
YEAH.

BOOM

WITH HUMBLE RESPECT, IF YOU **TELL US** WHAT YOUR, UM, PURPOSE IS, WE WILL LEAVE YOU ALONE AND, UM, IN PEACE.

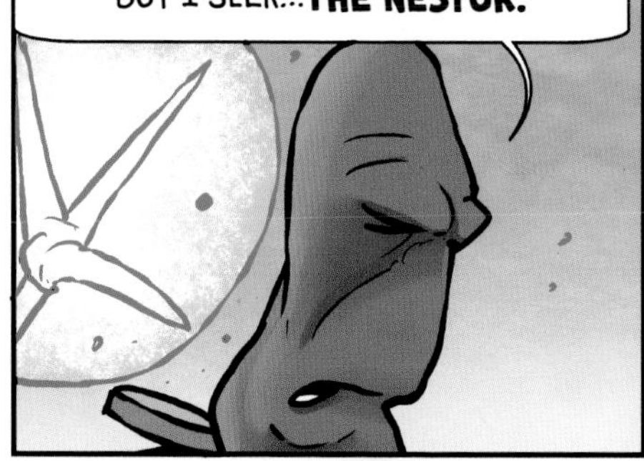
IT IS **TRULY** NONE OF YOUR CONCERN, BUT I SEEK... **THE NESTOR.**

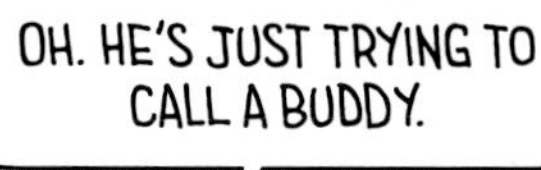
OH. HE'S JUST TRYING TO CALL A BUDDY.

ONCE FOUND, THE NESTOR WILL BE DESTROYED.

STILL RUDE.
YEAH.

NO ONE IS DESTROYING **ANYONE.**

PLECK

HEY!
OUTSTANDING! AN EXTRA ARM.

THE NESTOR **MUST** BE DESTROYED.
YOU WILL NOT DELAY ME!

GRACK

DID YOU--?
OH. NO. I FORGOT. I CAN'T DO THAT ANYMORE.

IT WAS GINA.
STOP.
I WON'T ASK YOU AGAIN.

NO! I WILL HAVE MY PREY! I WILL DESTROY THE NESTOR.

ZAP

SPLORCH

AAAAAAAAAAAAAAAAAAAAAAAAAAAAAAAAAA
GEEEEEEEN

KICK

MAY I COME DOWN? I AM NOT PARTICULARLY COMFORTABLE WITH HEIGHTS! **PLEASE!**

IT'S A **LITTLE** LATE TO START BEING NICE!
WHAT DO YOU SUPPOSE THIS THING IS?
DON'T KNOW. BUT IT SMELLS LIKE A POSSUM'S BUTT.

I'LL LET YOU DOWN, BUT YOU HAVE TO TELL US WHAT YOU'RE DOING.

YOU HAVE MY WORD.

THANK YOU! I AM MOST GRATEFUL! **THANK YOU!**

NOW! TO BEST EXPLAIN, PLEASE STUDY THE TOP OF THE OBJECT...

AW, DUDE.

FWUP

YOU FORGOT THAT YOU CAN'T FLY ANYMORE.
I FORGOT THAT I CAN'T FLY ANYMORE.

POOF

DANG IT. MAYBE YOU COULD DO A **SPELL** THAT MIGHT HELP YOU FIGURE OUT WHAT IT WAS.

IF I COULD STILL FLY, I WOULD HAVE **TOTALLY** CAUGHT THAT GUY.
TOTALLY.

YEAH. WE'RE DONE HERE.

WHAT?

YEP. **IT'S** GONE. **HE'S** GONE. **THE PROBLEM** IS GONE.
I'M GONE.

IT'S DONE.

SHE IS NOT NERVOUS ANYMORE.

CHAPTER 4

RAH

YES, DAD. **DUH.** IT HAS ALL KINDS OF CATEGORIES.
IT'S ONLY THE BIGGEST DIVISION FOUR, UNDERGRAD, NON-SCHOLASTIC, MID-REGIONAL CHEERLEADING COMPETITION. DUH.

DO NOT **DUH** YOUR FATHER.

SORRY.

WELL, THAT SOUNDS EXCITING.
IT TOTALLY IS.
TOTALLY.

CAN **I** DO IT?

WHAT?
YEAH--**WHAT?**

CAN I JOIN YOU TWO? CAN I CHEER WITH YOU?

RAH!

GINA. YOU GAVE UP CHEERLEADING. I THOUGHT YOU DIDN'T WANT TO DO IT ANYMORE.

ARE YOU MAKING FUN OF US?
SHE'S MAKING FUN OF US.
TOTALLY MAKING FUN OF US.

I'M NOT. I MEAN IT!

GINA.

WHAT?! I CAN'T CHANGE MY MIND?! MAYBE I WANT TO DO SOMETHING, Y'KNOW--**FUN** LIKE THIS. **NORMAL** LIKE THIS.

RAH!

TOTALLY MAKING FUN OF US.
MOCKING US.
YES! WE ARE BEING MOCKED.

I'M NOT! WHY IS IT SO HARD TO BELIEVE THAT I MIGHT WANT TO BE A CHEERLEADER?!

RAH!

HEY.
HEY.

I WAS SERIOUS ABOUT THAT!
I COULD TELL.

I TOTALLY WAS SERIOUS, AND I WANT TO JOIN BONNIE AND CONNE IN THEIR CHEERLEADING GAME--TOURNAMENT--THING!

I BELIEVE YOU.

I'M JUST PRETTY CONFUSED AS TO **WHY** YOU WANT TO. ALL OF A SUDDEN.

I JUST DO.
UH-HUH.

YOU KNOW THAT YOU'RE NAMED AFTER MY GREAT-GREAT-GRANDMOTHER, RIGHT?

YES.

WHEN YOUR MOTHER WAS PREGNANT WITH YOU, MY GREAT-GRANDMOTHER PUT HER HANDS ON MOM'S BELLY AND SAID--
"REGINA! REGINA'S SPIRIT IS IN THERE!"

YES. EXCEPT, WELL, SHE CALLED HER BY HER NICKNAME. **MAMA REGGIE.**

REALLY? REGGIE?

YEAH. YOUR MOTHER DID NOT WANT YOU GOING BY "REGGIE." SO SHE ASKED ME NOT TO TELL YOU THAT.
BUT THE STORY GOES THAT REGGIE... WELL, SHE WAS SOMETHING ELSE.
I KNOW. YOU AND GRANDMA TOLD ME.
NOT ALL OF IT.
REGGIE HAD A JOB AT AN ANTIQUES STORE WHEN SHE WAS YOUR AGE. THE OWNERS LOVED HOW TOUGH SHE WAS.
THEY TOLD HER TO GROWL AT ANYONE WHO TOUCHED ANYTHING IN THE STORE.
YOU BREAK IT, YOU BOUGHT IT!
APPARENTLY, SHE SAID THAT HER ENTIRE LIFE. SHE WAS BIG ON TAKING RESPONSIBILITY.
YOU BREAK IT, YOU BOUGHT IT!

SHE RAISED THREE CHILDREN ON HER OWN.
TAUGHT HERSELF TO READ.
BECAME A TEACHER.
A GUIDE IN A MUSEUM.

AND SHE WAS FORMIDABLE.
WORD WAS TWO THIEVES BROKE INTO HER APARTMENT ONCE, AND REGGIE **BEAT** THEM SILLY.
YOU BETTER RUN!!

YEAH?
OH YEAH.

SHE DIED YOUNG, THOUGH. BUT SHE **LIVED.** Y'KNOW?

DAD. WHY ARE WE TALKING ABOUT MAMA REGGIE?

REGGIE KNEW WHO SHE WAS.

SO DO YOU.

WHY DO YOU ALWAYS GET THE **WEIRDEST** ONES?
I LIKE NEW THINGS.
ICE CREAM
BUT YOU GET THE WEIRDEST STUFF.
I'VE ONLY HAD HUMAN TASTE BUDS FOR A LITTLE WHILE, AND IT'S **FUN** TO GIVE THEM A WORKOUT!
WHAT FLAVOR DID YOU GET THIS TIME?
GRAPE BUBBLE-GUM ICE CREAM WITH JASMINE-COVERED RAISINS.
HOW DOES IT TASTE?
IT'S AWFUL. BUT IT'S **NEW.**
AND--
DON'T SAY IT--
TURNS MY POOP **PURPLE.**
OH!

PUT
PUT PUT
PUT
AND MY TONGUE!
DUDE!
TRY IT! IT'S TERRIBLE!
NO! AND IT'S GOT YOUR GERMS!
PUT PUT PUT PUT PUT
PUT PUT PUT
PUT
PUT
NO. I DON'T HAVE ANY GERMS THAT COULD BE TRANSMITTABLE.
TRY SOME!
WHAT? NO! AND--WHAT DO YOU MEAN, YOU DON'T HAVE ANY GERMS THAT--
WHAT? HEY--

YOU MAY **ASK,** MISSY, BUT I WON'T BE TELLIN'.

I DIDN'T THINK YOU HUMANS COULD **SEE** US MAGICAL FOLKS. WHAT D'THEY CALL YA?

MY NAME'S GINA COOPER.

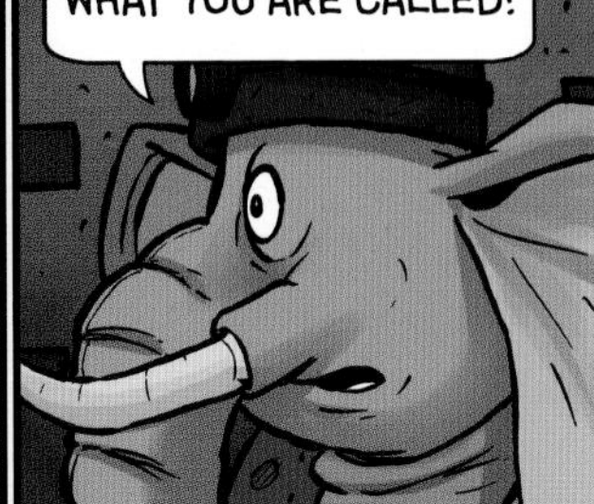
WHOA! I DIDN'T ASK YER **NAME**--I ASKED WHAT YOU ARE CALLED!

THE OLDEST, SIMPLEST, MOST SACRED RULE OF MAGIC IS THAT YER **PROPER NAME** HAS **POWER!** YOU DON'T JUS' **GIVE** IT AWAY!

I DON'T THINK THE "RULE" MATTERS TO ME. BECAUSE, WELL... I REALLY DON'T **WANT** TO DO MAGIC ANYMORE.

YOU DON'T REALLY HAVE A **CHOICE.** YOU CAN'T CHOOSE **WHAT** YA ARE.
ONLY **WHO** YOU'LL BE.

SNIIIF

OOF! I'VE GOT THE SCENT! THE **NESTOR'S** NEAR!
YOU'RE LOOKING FOR THE NESTOR TOO?
CLICK

NOT LOOKING!

FOUND!

PIZZA
HARDWARE
TZOT
TZOT
LOOKS LIKE YER STILL IN THE MAGIC, GINA COOPER!
EXAMINER
NEWS

RK

THE NESTOR?

CREEOK

SPLORCH

SKIIIIIIID

BLARP BLARP BLARP BLARP
BLARP

WHUMP
SKIIIID

FREEZE, FURBALLS!

GRRRRRRRRRRRRRRR

HOOOOOOOOOOOOOORC

OH, BOY.

BLOOOOORCH

UCK.
DOG LOOGIE.

BLAARP
BLAARP
BLARP
BLARP
BLAARP

SPLASH

SPLASH

SPLASH

SPLOORCH

WHUUMP

HOLY MACKEREL!

GINA, WHAT ARE YOU DOING IN THE WATER?

WHAT ARE YOU WEARING?
TIGHTS! LIKE **SPIDER-MAN!**

WE SENSED THERE WAS TROUBLE, AND WE HOPPED INTO ACTION.

POOF

MAN. THEY DISAPPEARED.
JUST LIKE THAT STAFF THINGY.

DO YOU THINK THEY'RE **TELEPORTING** AWAY, OR ARE THE DOGS **THEMSELVES** SOME KIND OF SPELL?

IT DOESN'T MATTER.

DON'T YOU WANT TO TRY TO FIGURE OUT WHAT'S GOING ON?

NO.
THEY'RE GONE. I'M GONE.

IT'S DONE.

I THINK WE SHOULD ALL WEAR TIGHTS.
NO.

HELP

HILO LOOKED UP SOME STUFF.

HE'S BEEN DOING RESEARCH. HE **ACTUALLY** FOUND SOME BOOKS ABOUT **MAGIC** THAT DON'T SOUND TOTALLY WEIRD.

AND HE MADE US ALL **TIGHTS.**

AND A MANGO SALAD. THE SALAD IS GOOD.

I DON'T NEED TO KNOW ANYTHING ABOUT MAGIC.

THEN HOW ARE WE GOING TO FIGURE OUT WHY ALL THESE **CREATURES** ARE POPPING UP?

WE AREN'T. **I'M** NOT. **NO ONE** IS GOING TO BE INVESTIGATING OR FIGHTING OR TRYING TO STOP **ANYONE** OR ANY **MAGIC.**

I'M NOT DOING IT.

BUT WE **HAVE** TO. IF **WE** DON'T, WHO WILL?

THE POLICE! THE ARMY! THE GOVERNMENT!

THEY DON'T KNOW ABOUT MAGIC. THEY CAN'T EVEN **SEE** MAGIC. **YOU'RE** THE ONLY ONE WHO CAN.

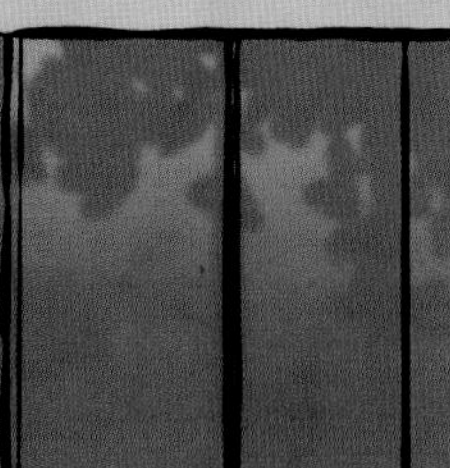

NO.
WHY?
I DON'T **WANT** TO.
WHY?
STOP ASKING ME.
NO. **WHY** WON'T YOU DO THIS?
BECAUSE IZZY DIED!

WHEN WE WERE "BEING SUPERHEROES." WHEN WE WERE FIGHTING BAD GUYS...

SHE DIED.

I MISS HER TOO.

BUT IT WASN'T YOUR FAULT.
IT WASN'T **MY** FAULT. OR **HILO'S.** IT HAPPENED. SHE DIED TO SAVE EVERYONE.

SHE DIED HELPING HILO.

YES.

I'M NOT HILO OR IZZY.

THEY HAD SUPERPOWERS. THEY **HAD** TO FIGHT TO SAVE THEIR WORLD.

YOU HAVE POWERS.

I DON'T EVEN KNOW WHAT I'M DOING, D.J.
AND THESE MAGICAL FOLKS COULD BE DANGEROUS.

I DON'T WANT ANY OF YOU TO GET HURT.

YOU WOULDN'T LET ANYTHING HAPPEN TO US.

YOU DON'T KNOW THAT.

I **DO.**

HOOM

POLLY...

I NEED HELP...

POLLY...

CREEEEN
PELE
PELE

THAT'S WHY I DECIDED TO DEFINITELY GET A UNICYCLE.
Vanderbilt Elementary School

YOU DON'T THINK THAT HAT IS ENOUGH?
NOPE. NEW ME. NEW STUFF.

A UNICYCLE. AND MAYBE GROW A MUSTACHE.

YOU CAN'T GROW A MUSTACHE.
NOT IF I DON'T TRY!

SOMETHING IN GINA'S BAG JUST GOT SIXTEEN DEGREES HOTTER.

WHAT?
HOW DO YOU KNOW THAT?

NOW IT'S EIGHTEEN DEGREES HOTTER.

WHAT'S THAT?
IT'S A CRYSTAL BALL! WHAT'S IT SAYING?

WHERE'D YOU GET THAT?
I, Y'KNOW, MAGICKED IT. BY ACCIDENT.

LOOK!
THAT'S THE **SOCCER FIELD** AT THE HIGH SCHOOL.

MAYBE WE'RE SUPPOSED TO GO THERE!

NO! **I'M** SUPPOSED TO GO THERE!

WE'RE COMING TOO!
I HAVE OUR TIGHTS!

OH, BOY.

I GUESS THAT'S WHY WE'RE HERE.
YEAH. C'MON!

WE'D BE GOING A LOT FASTER IF WE ALL HAD UNICYCLES!

CLACK

WUUUMP

THOSE ARE GREAT HATS.

NESTOR

NESTOR. THEY SAID NESTOR.
YEAH. WHO IS THE NESTOR?

CREEEEE

HEEEEEEM

WOW! I DID **NOT** SEE THAT COMING!!
LOOK!

THERE!
THE NESTOR!

NESTOR!!

C'MON!
I THOUGHT YOU DIDN'T WANT TO DO THIS ANYMORE!
I DON'T!

BUT I DON'T REALLY HAVE A **CHOICE!**

WHATEVER THE **NESTOR** IS, I DON'T THINK IT'S RIGHT THAT WE JUST LET IT GET CAPTURED OR DESTROYED!

I BET THOSE LADIES WHO TURNED INTO THAT CATERPILLAR ARE **WITCHES** FROM THE **CLAN OF BABA YAGA!**
WHAT?!

I READ THIS BOOK OF MAGIC. IT WAS IN ANCIENT **EAST SLAVIC,** BUT--
YOU CAN **READ** ANCIENT EAST SLAVIC?

YEAH! CAN'T YOU?!
FOCUS! WHAT DID IT SAY?!

BABA YAGA CLAN MEMBERS--OR, AS I LIKE TO CALL THEM, **BAB YAGS!**-- AREN'T **NATURAL** SHAPE-SHIFTERS!

THEY NEED A **MAGIC TOTEM** OR AN **AMULET** THAT ENABLES THEM TO TRANSMOGRIFY!

GOT IT! I THINK!

TZEEN
GET AWAY FROM THE NESTOR!

ROAR

OH. IS **THAT** THE NESTOR?

THERE'S **TWO** OF THEM.
THEY'RE SO **LITTLE.**

YOU GET THEM. **I'LL** GET HER.
BUT WE CAN HELP!

YOU ARE! **YOU** GET **THEM--**

I'LL GET HER!
EEP
TZOT

CRUD!
ROOAR

WE'RE HERE TO HELP!

CAN YOU TELL THEM WE'RE HERE TO HELP?!
YEP!

WE'RE HERE TO HELP!

DUDE. I MEANT IF YOU COULD SPEAK THEIR LANGUAGE. I FIGURED YOU CAN READ ANCIENT EAST SLAVIC--

BLAM

AAAAAAAAAAAAA

I THINK THEY'RE SCARED AND WANT US TO RUN AWAY!
I GOT THAT!
AAAAAAAAAAAAA

ROOOOOAR

ROOAARR
AAAAAAAAAAA

HWIIIIIIIP

AW. I **REALLY** DIDN'T THINK THIS THROUGH.

HWAAAANG
AAAA
AAAH

CRUNK

SKIIIIIIIIIIIIID

AAAAAAA AA AAAAAAA

AAAA AAAAA
PARK

CAN PEOPLE **SEE** WHAT WE'RE HOLDING?!
THESE PUPPIES ARE MAGICAL! PROBABLY NOT!

SO?!
YEAH!

WE LOOK PRETTY WEIRD!

AAAAAA
AAAAAAH!

FLECK

PLOORK

THAT'S NOT GOOD.

CRUD.
FLUMP

HOLY MACKEREL.

I WISH THERE WAS SOME WAY WE COULD **UNDERSTAND** THEM!
YEAH! LET ME TRY SOMETHING!

DO YOU SPEAK ENGLISH?!
YES.

THIS ONE SPEAKS ENGLISH.
I GOT THAT.

TUCK TUCK TUCK

RIP

CLICK

ZAP

CRACK

AAAAAAAAAAAH!

BLAM!

HELLO, MAGICAL AMULET.

GOODBYE, MAGICAL SPELL.
SNAP.

WELCOME BACK, BAB YAGS.
BWEEEEEE

POOF

MUCH THANKS, HUMAN BEING. WE ARE **ETERNALLY** IN YOUR DEBT.
THIS ONE SPEAKS ENGLISH.
I GOT THAT.

LET'S GO HOME.

YOU FELLAS WANT TIGHTS?

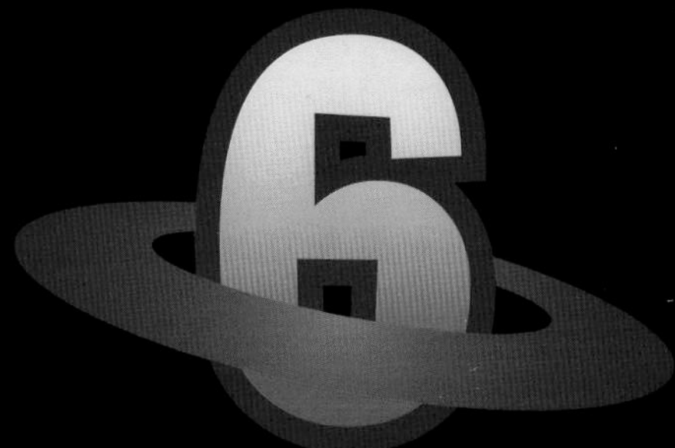

WE CARRY WHO THEY WERE

GINA?

OH! HEY, MOM!

WHAT ARE YOU KIDS UP TO?

WELL, WE ARE **TOTALLY** NOT SNEAKING TWO MAGICAL BEINGS INTO YOUR HOUSE TO HIDE THEM FROM OTHER MAGICAL BEINGS WHO ARE HUNTING THEM.

YOU ARE A VERY STRANGE CHILD, AND I LOVE YOU.

SEE YA, MOM.
I LOVE YOU TOO, MRS. COOPER!

I AM **SO** GOOD AT COVERING UP OUR STUFF NOW.

SO?

YOU SPEAK ENGLISH?
YES. I TOOK A CLASS.
AND HE LEARNED TO KNIT.

AND HE MIGHT MAKE ME A **HAT.**
YES.

YOU DON'T SPEAK ENGLISH?
NO.

I AM CALLED **BEK.** AND HE IS CALLED **CHOI.**

BOK AND CHOY? LIKE THE VEGETABLE?
BOK CHOY! THOSE ARE DELICIOUS!

NO. **BEK** AND **CHOI.** AND **NO,** CHOI, THEY ARE **NOT** GOING TO EAT US.

YOU ARE **NOT** GOING TO EAT US?

NO!

COULD YOU **PLEASE** JUST TELL US WHAT'S GOING ON? AND WHY YOU'RE BEING CHASED?

AND MAYBE WHY FOLKS WANT TO DESTROY YOU?
THAT TOO.

MANGO?
YES.

WE ARE **NESTOR.** WE ARE AMONG THE LAST OF OUR KIND.

TENS OF THOUSANDS OF YEARS AGO, WE WERE **PLENTIFUL** AND WERE LEFT TO LIVE IN PEACE.

TO BEINGS WHO DO MAGIC, IT MUST HAVE MADE THEM VERY...

VALUABLE.

YES.

YOU WERE HUNTED.

FOR THOUSANDS OF YEARS WE HAVE BEEN **CAPTURED** AND USED TO MAKE MAGICAL BEINGS MORE POWERFUL.

MANY SOUGHT TO **DESTROY** US IN ORDER TO ROB **OTHERS** OF THE OPPORTUNITY TO BE STRONGER.

AND **THAT'S** WHO'S CHASING YOU NOW? MAGICAL BEINGS WHO DON'T WANT YOU TO HELP **OTHER** MAGICAL BEINGS?

YES.
BUT WE JUST WANT TO REJOIN OUR PEOPLE.

WE WANT TO GO **HOME.**

HOW CAN WE HELP?

THE NESTOR ARE **MUCH** LESS NERVOUS NOW.

HOW DO YOU KNOW **THAT?**

I FELT THEIR **BLOOD PRESSURE** GO DOWN.

COULDN'T YOU?

NO.

OH.

THEY'RE HUNGRY. CAN YOU FEEL **THAT?**

NO!

I MIGHT **STILL** BE ABLE TO DO SOME OTHER STUFF YOU CAN'T.

THAT'S BANANAS.

YOU KNOW WHEN SOMEONE'S SKIN **TEMPERATURE** GOES UP OR DOWN? YOU CAN SEE IN THE **DARK?** AND...YOU DON'T **SLEEP?**
NOT A LOT.

GESUNDHEIT.

AH CHOO

OH YEAH. I ALSO KNOW WHEN SOMEONE IS GOING TO **SNEEZE.**

WHY DIDN'T YOU **TELL** US YOU COULD DO ALL THIS STUFF?

I DIDN'T KNOW IT WAS **IMPORTANT.** I THOUGHT MOSTLY **EVERYBODY** WAS LIKE THIS.

IT WASN'T LIKE THERE'S A BOOK ON HOW TO BE HUMAN.

GESUNDHEIT.

AH-CHOO

SO. MAYBE YOU'RE NOT EXACTLY HUMAN.

NO. I THINK I AM.

I THINK I JUST HAVE **IZZY** IN ME.

WHAT?

WELL...

WHEN IZZY GAVE ME ALL OF HER ENERGY, **PARTS** OF HER GOT INSIDE ME TOO.

IZZY WAS SMARTER THAN ME. SMARTER THAN **EVERYONE.** SHE COULD DO THINGS WITH MACHINES. SHE UNDERSTOOD COMPUTERS. AND FOR HER, **PEOPLE** WERE A LOT LIKE MACHINES.

SHE KNEW HOW PEOPLE WORK. SHE COULD **SEE** HOW THEIR BODIES WERE WORKING **JUST** LIKE SHE SAW MACHINES.

NOW...**I** CAN TOO.

YOU CAN **FEEL** IZZY INSIDE YOU.

NOT EXACTLY. BUT I **FEEL** HER. I FEEL LIKE SHE'S WATCHING ME. WATCHING **US.**

SOME DAYS... IT'S LIKE I CAN FEEL HER SITTING RIGHT BESIDE ME.

SNIFF.

YOUR MOM SAID THAT HAPPENS.

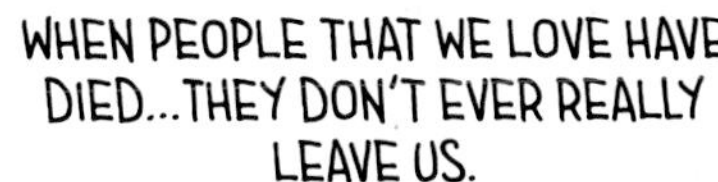
WHEN PEOPLE THAT WE LOVE HAVE DIED...THEY DON'T EVER REALLY LEAVE US.

WE **CARRY** WHO THEY WERE.

INSIDE US.

BUT I GUESS I CARRY MORE THAN MOST PEOPLE.

I'M LUCKY.

I MISS HER.

BUT SHE'S STILL RIGHT NEXT TO ME.

CHAPTER

RARE AND SPECIAL

HOW CAN YOU GET HOME?

THERE WILL BE A **GATE.**

A **DOOR.**
A **PORTAL.**
WHERE'S THE GATE?

WHERE IS LESS IMPORTANT THAN **WHEN.**

OH. IT'S LIKE A BUS. THAT GATE SHOWS UP ON A **SCHEDULE.**

WHEN IS THE BUS COMING, AND WHERE IS THE BUS STOP?

SUNDOWN TOMORROW. THAT BIG HILL NEXT TO WAGNER LAKE.

YOU CAN UNDERSTAND HIM NOW?
PRETTY MUCH.

SHRIMP CRACKER?

OKAY. SO WE JUST HAVE TO HIDE THEM UNTIL TOMORROW.

THAT SHOULDN'T BE TOO HARD SINCE THEY'RE **INVISIBLE** TO HUMANS.

THAT **IS** TRUE.
REALLY?

GINA! MOM WANTS TO KNOW IF YOUR POSSE OF **NERDS** IS STAYING FOR DINNER.

KICK
SLAM

GET UNDER THE BED!
ABSOLUTELY!

WHAT IS A **BED?**
WHAT'S WRONG?

WE HAVE CONSUMED **FOOD** OF THIS PLANET. IT MAKES US VISIBLE.

YOU DID **NOT** JUST SLAM THE DOOR IN MY FACE!
YES, SHE **DID!**

SORRY! IT WAS THE WIND. MY BAD! **YES!** MY FRIENDS ARE STAYING FOR DINNER. **MAYBE!** LEMME GET BACK TO YOU.

SLAM

SHE SLAMMED THE DOOR ON YOU **AGAIN.**
RUDE.
WAY RUDE.

OKAY. WE HAVE TO KEEP THESE FELLAS SAFE **AND** SECRET UNTIL SUNDOWN TOMORROW NIGHT.

WAY RUDE.

WE GOTTA EMPTY OUT THIS HOUSE.

YOU GOT THIS?
OH, YES.

HACKING COMPUTERS ISN'T THAT HARD. FOR ME.

HOW LONG WILL IT TAKE?

CLICK

EEEEEEEEEEE!

I'M DONE.

WE GOT IN!
WE GOT IN!!

WE HAVE BEEN CHOSEN FOR THE DIVISION FOUR, UNDERGRAD, NON-SCHOLASTIC, MID-REGIONAL **CHEERLEADING COMPETITION!**

EEEEEEEE!

CONGRATULATIONS.
WHEN IS IT?

TOMORROW!
TOTALLY TOMORROW!

WELL, I **GUESS--**
BOTH YOU AND DAD **HAVE** TO COME!

MOM! YOU NEED TO BE ON THE FLOOR WITH US!
DAD! YOU HAVE TO VIDEO **ALL** OF OUR PERFORMANCES!
ALL?

THERE'S PRELIMINARIES!
SECONDARY PRELIMINARIES!
PRELIMINARY SEMIFINALS!
SECONDARY SEMIFINALS!
YOU HAVE TO FILM THEM **ALL!**

AND WE HAVE TO CHANGE OUTFITS FOR EACH ROUND! **DUH!**
WHY ARE WE STILL **STANDING** HERE?

WHY AREN'T YOU PACKING?!

WE MAY HAVE TO RENT A TRUCK!

YES.
RIGHT
THERE.
GINA'S
ROOM

YOU SURE THIS IS WHERE THE GATE WILL BE?
WE HAVE CHECKED THE CALCULATIONS AGAIN AND AGAIN.

THIS GATE WILL RETURN US TO OUR HOME. OUR PEOPLE. **THIS** IS WHERE WE NESTOR BEGAN.

BUT WE ARE **SO** VERY SORRY FOR THE TROUBLES WE HAVE CAUSED, GINA COOPER...AND ANY TROUBLES WE **MAY** CAUSE.

IT'S OKAY. I'M GLAD I CAN HELP.

WE ARE GLAD AND LUCKY TO HAVE FOUND AN ACTUAL **ENCHANTER** ON **EARTH.**
YES. A **MIRACLE.**

WELL, IT'S NOT **THAT.** MY FRIEND **POLLY** JUST SHOWED ME I COULD DO SOME MAGIC.

IT'S **NOT** "SOME MAGIC." YOU ARE NOT JUST A **WIZARD** WHO HAS TO RECITE SPELLS.

YOU HAVE **NO** MAGICAL TOOLS. OR BOOKS. OR CHARMS.
YOU ARE AN **ENCHANTER.** YOU DRAW MAGIC FROM THE **PLANET** ITSELF. YOU **MAKE** MAGIC.

THAT IS RARE. AND SPECIAL.
YES. UNTIL **YOU,** THERE HAS BEEN NO MAGIC ON EARTH IN **100,000 YEARS.**
THERE USED TO BE MAGIC ON **EARTH?**

OH, YES. BUT THERE WERE CONCERNS THAT IT WOULD TOO GREATLY INTERFERE WITH A "NEW" FORM OF LIFE.
HUMANS.
SO MAGIC **REMOVED** ITSELF FROM THIS WORLD.
YES.
THE NESTOR WERE HERE ON THIS WORLD. IT WAS A **SIMPLER** TIME FOR ALL.
BUT **I'M** DOING MAGIC ON EARTH. AND THERE'S--

YES. GATES OPENING. MAGICAL BEINGS AFOOT.

YOU, GINA COOPER, HAVE OPENED A DOOR THAT HAS BEEN LONG CLOSED.

YOU MAY HAVE BROUGHT MAGIC BACK TO EARTH.

CHAPTER

ADVENTURES IN BABYSITTING

MY FAMILY WILL BE LEAVING IN A MINUTE.

MY FRIENDS ARE COMING OVER, AND **ALL** WE HAVE TO DO IS HANG HERE UNTIL SUNDOWN.

THEN YOU WILL
HELP US GET HOME?

THEN I WILL HELP
YOU GET HOME.

BREEENG
D.J.
GUT

HEY! WHERE ARE YOU?

YEAH. WE'RE COMING UP YOUR STREET.

BUT I WANTED TO GIVE
YOU A HEADS-UP--

WE NEED TO GO NOW!!

TELL ME WHEN YOU GET HERE. LOUD DRAMA IS HAPPENING.

WE ARE GOING TO BE **LATE!**
WE **CANNOT** BE LATE!
YOU ARE GOING TO HAVE TO STOP YELLING AT ME.

WE **AREN'T** YELLING! THIS IS JUST VOLUME!

SO EXCITED!
SO NERVOUS!
AND **NERVOUS!**

THERE'S **ADRENALINE** BLASTING THROUGH US LIKE A **TORNADO!**

BONNIE IS HYPERVENTILATING!
WE!
EEEEEEEEEFFF

NEED!
HOOF

TO!
EEEF

LEAVE!
HOOF

DING DONG
AAAAAH!

RELAX! IT'S JUST D.J. I GOT IT!
I'M HAVING A HEART ATTACK!

HEY! **LISA!** YOU CAME OVER TOO?

WELL. YES. I THOUGHT I MIGHT BE ABLE TO HELP.

THANKS! BUT, TO BE HONEST, THESE LITTLE MAGIC FELLAS ARE **PRETTY** CHILL.

YEAH. I DIDN'T MEAN HELP WITH THEM.

SUP, GINA.

WHAT IS **DEXTER** DOING HERE?

WHAT IS THEIR BROTHER DEXTER DOING HERE?

WELL, YOU DIDN'T THINK WE WERE GOING TO LEAVE YOU IN THE HOUSE **ALL DAY** BY **YOURSELVES,** DID YOU?

I DID. I **DID** ACTUALLY THINK THAT. WE DON'T NEED A BABYSITTER.

YOU DON'T. BUT I WOULDN'T CONSIDER THIS **BABYSITTING.** MORE LIKE "TEENAGE SUPERVISION."

EXACTLY. NOTHING TO WORRY ABOUT HERE, MRS. COOPER. WE ARE JUST GOING TO HANG OUT. YOU ALL HAVE A GOOD TIME.

THANK YOU, DEXTER. WE--

HOOOONK

WE NEED TO GO!!
YOU MUST CHILL!

BYE! GOOD LUCK, LADIES! DON'T WORRY ABOUT US!

SLAM

OKAY, DORKS, HERE'S THE DEAL.

I AM IN CHARGE. MY WORD IS THE **LAW.** I HAVE A TERM PAPER I NEED TO WORK ON AND--
YOU HAVE TO BE QUIET.

OKAY. GREAT. WE'LL BE IN MY ROOM.

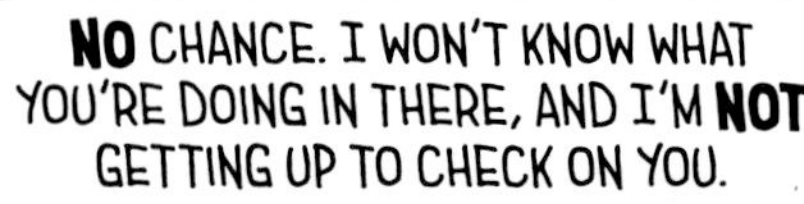
NO CHANCE. I WON'T KNOW WHAT YOU'RE DOING IN THERE, AND I'M NOT GETTING UP TO CHECK ON YOU.

I WILL BE HERE. AT THE TABLE. WORKING.

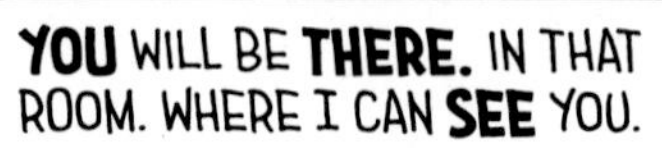
YOU WILL BE THERE. IN THAT ROOM. WHERE I CAN SEE YOU.

THAT'S NOT REALLY FAIR.

TOUGH TURKEY. IT'S A LIFE LESSON. THINGS AREN'T FAIR. DO HOMEWORK. READ A BOOK. STARE INTO SPACE. BUT DO IT QUIETLY.

IN THAT ROOM. WHERE I CAN SEE YOU.

HOW COULD YOU LET THIS HAPPEN?!
WE DIDN'T **LET** THIS HAPPEN. **YOUR** MOM CALLED AND ASKED IF HE'D COME OVER.

WHAT ABOUT **YOUR** MOM! SHE **KNOWS** ABOUT HILO AND MAGIC AND EVERYTHING. **YOU** COULD HAVE TOLD HER ABOUT THE MAGICAL PEEPS! **SHE** WOULD'VE HELPED US!

WE THOUGHT OF THAT. BUT SHE'S ON A **PLANE** FLYING TO FLORIDA TO SEE OUR **AUNT HELEN.**
HELEN BROKE HER ANKLE WATER-SKIING.

ISN'T YOUR AUNT HELEN, LIKE, **80** YEARS OLD?
YES. WHICH IS **WHY** SHE BROKE HER ANKLE WHEN SHE WENT WATERSKIING.

AUNT HELEN IS THE **BOMB.** SHE SKATEBOARDS **AND** STARTED KICKBOXING. SHE'S GETTING INTO TATTOOS. SHE'S **GNARLY.**

A LITTLE QUIETER IN THERE!

SORRY!

THIS IS **NOT** GONNA WORK. WE HAVE **GOT** TO GET BACK TO MY ROOM TO CHECK ON THE NESTOR.

NO. IT'S OKAY. THEY'RE HERE.

HELLO! WE ARE HUNGRY.

WHAT? **WHO** SAID THAT?

WHAT'S GOING ON?

DEXTER! CHECK IT!

THERE'S A FACE ON MY BELLY! WATCH HER WHISTLE!!

TOOT TOOT!

SIT **DOWN,** DORK. WHERE'S GINA?

BATHROOM!
KITCHEN!

GINA! WHERE'D YOU GO?!

I WENT TO THE KITCHEN, **THEN** THE BATHROOM!!

TOOT TOOT!
I **SAID** SIT DOWN!
GINA, GET BACK IN HERE!

WHEN DID YOU DRAW A **FACE** ON YOUR STOMACH?
I DRAW A FACE ON MY STOMACH **A LOT.** YOU NEVER KNOW WHEN YOU'RE GONNA NEED ONE.

TOOT!

TOOT!
GET OUT OF MY WAY, DORKUS!!

VIDEO GAMES!

WHAT?

CAN WE PLAY VIDEO GAMES?

OH.

YOU STILL PRETTY GOOD AT WORLD OF PLANET MONGER FURY 8?

PRETTY GOOD? NO.

I AM A MASTER.

I'M **NOT** GONNA LISTEN TO WHATEVER **DANCING BABY ANIMAL** IDIOCY **YOU** CALL A VIDEO GAME WHILE--

IS THAT...

PLANET MONGER
FURY
8
START
SELECT
YOU'RE PLAYING **WORLD OF PLANET MONGER FURY 8?**

HERE WE GO...

YUP. I'M PRETTY GOOD. I'VE MADE IT ALL THE WAY TO **LEVEL TWO.**

LEVEL **TWO?** YOU'RE **BRAGGING** ABOUT MAKING IT TO THE **DARK HIGHLANDS OF THE KINGDOM OF RUK?**

I MADE IT TO LEVEL TWO ON MY **FIRST** ROUND **WITHOUT** EVEN MASTERING THE CONTROLLER SETTINGS YET!

DO YOU WANT TO PLAY? I KNOW YOU HAVE **SO** MUCH--

I WILL BE SELECTING **MALACHI THE DESTROYER** AS MY AVATAR!
BOOP

OKAY, I'LL BE--
WHATEVER! HIT START! START! START! START!

PLANET MONGER FURY!

HE IS PROBABLY LOOKING AROUND. HE IS NATURALLY CURIOUS.

GRRR. EEERRH!
TAP TAP TAP TAP
TAP TAP TAP TAP
HAVING TROUBLE?

I'M **FINE!!**
TAP TAP TAP TAP TAP
TAP TAP TAP TAP TAP

AAAAH!
TAP TAP
TAP TAP TAP TAP TAP TAP TAP
BOOP

TAP TAP
TAP TAP TAP TAP TAP TAP TAP TAP
WOW. LOOK. I JUST SCORED A **BATTLE ARMOR UPGRADE** FOR MY **WHOLE** DIVISION. AND **YOU** LOST YOUR **WHOLE** DARK ELF SQUAD.

THAT WAS LUCK!
TAP TAP TAP TAP TAP TAP
TAP TAP TAP TAP
UH-HUH.

WHAT WAS THA--
BOOP
HOOOOOW DID YOU EARN A BONUS VOLCANIC AIRSHIP CHARGER?!
AAAAAH!

I AM **MOST** SORRY FOR THE TROUBLE.
ALL GOOD. LET'S JUST GET TO GINA'S ROOM.

WHOA!

HOW DID YOU GET SO **BIG?**

I **MAY** HAVE PUT EXTRA FOOD IN MY POUCH.

YOU HAVE A **POUCH,** AND YOU FILLED IT WITH **CANNED GOODS?**

SO AWESOME, WEIRD, **AND** BRILLIANT. KEEP MOVING.

IT'S CALLED A **BASEMENT.** IT'S BENEATH THE HOUSE. AND PEOPLE KEEP **ALL** KINDS OF STUFF IN THEM.

WHOA! YEAH! LIKE THIS **ROCKING** DRUM SET!

WILL YOU BOTH KEEP IT DOWN?! WE'RE **TRYING** TO HIDE FROM DEXTER!
WHO'S THE MUSICIAN IN GINA'S FAMILY?

HER MOM AND DAD PLAY. BUT **LOOK,** WE JUST NEED TO QUIETLY SNEAK BACK INTO GINA'S ROOM. SO, LET'S CREEP UP THE--
BOO-DO BOP BOO-DO CRASH

CHOI! STOP!! HOLY MACKEREL! STOP!
BOOM BA BOOM DAH
BO

HILO, WILL YOU **PLEASE** HELP?!

YEP! I'M IN!
BWAANG

NO!
BWAAAAG

WILL YOU TURN THAT MUSIC **OFF?!** I CAN'T CONCENTRATE!
TAP TAP TAP TAP TAP TAP TAP
BOOM DA BOOM
TAP TAP TAP TAP

TAP TAP TAP TAP TAP TAP TAP
TAP TAP TAP

DO YOU NEED TO GO TO THE **BATHROOM?**

NO!
TAP TAP TAP
TAP TAP TAP TAP TAP TAP

TAP TAP
TAP TAP TAP TAP TAP

I THINK YOU **DO.**

GAMER RULES! IF YOU **LEAK,** YOU'RE **WEAK!**
TAP TAP
TAP
TAP
TAP
TAP
TAP
TAP
TAP

TAP TAP
TAP
TAP
TAP

I'M WILLING TO **PAUSE** THE GAME AND LET YOU TAKE A BATHROOM BREAK.

TAP
TAP
TAP
TAP
TAP
TAP

AAAH! FINE!

BA DOOM BA BOOM
BWAAAAANNG

WHAT ARE YOU DOING?!

TEARING OUT A SWEET JAM.
I WAS TRYING TO GET THEM TO STOP, BUT THEN IT STARTED TO SOUND **REALLY** GOOD.

EVERYBODY. GET TO MY ROOM--**RIGHT NOW--**

BEFORE SOMETHING **ELSE** GOES HORRIBLY WRONG.

SOMETHING ELSE GOES HORRIBLY WRONG

INSIDE! GO!
HE WANTS TO GO BACK AND FINISH OUR SET.

HE'S RIGHT. WE **WERE** IN THE ZONE.
IT'S TRUE.

WE ARE SEEING HOW MUCH STUFF WE CAN FIT IN BEK'S POUCH!
IT **IS** ACTUALLY QUITE EXHILARATING.

HE'S GOT A **POUCH?!**
I **KNOW,** RIGHT?

HEY!

OKAY.

EVERYONE IS **PRETTY** EXCITED FOR DIFFERENT REASONS, BUT WE ARE **FORGETTING** OUR GOAL.

THESE TWO NEED TO GO TO A MAGICAL GATE TO GET HOME.

WE NEED TO KEEP THEM SAFE UNTIL SUNDOWN, WHEN THAT GATE IS READY TO OPEN.

AND RIGHT **NOW...** OUR TOP OF THE LIST, **MOST** IMPORTANT GOAL... IS TO MAKE SURE THAT **DEXTER** DOESN'T FIND OUT ABOUT **ANY** OF THIS.

HE'S STANDING RIGHT BEHIND ME, ISN'T HE?

YES.
YEP.
HEY, DEXTER!

Gina's ROOM
OKAY. DEXTER. JUST TRY TO STAY CALM.
AAAAA AAAH!!
AAAAAAAAH!!
OH, DEXTER, GET A GRIP.
HE MIGHT BE OKAY IF WE LET HIM SCREAM IT OUT FOR A BIT.

CLICKA

SCREEEEEE

DO YOU FEEL SOMETHING?

NO...BUT I FEEL THAT **YOU** FEEL SOMETHING

CRA
CRACKLE

LOOK OUT!!

BLOOOOON

HWAAANK

CRACKLE
CROOOOM

TZOT

BOOM

SKKIIIII

DDD
BREEEEN
YOU ALL OKAY?!

EVERYONE?! IS EVERYONE OKAY?!
YES.
YEAH.
I GUESS SO.

THANKS TO YOU. HOW DID YOU DO THIS?!

WHY AM I A **FERRET?!**
YOU ARE AN **OTTER.**

YOU TURNED ME INTO AN OTTER?

NO. BUT WE NESTOR **NATURALLY** INCREASE MAGICAL POWER. IT IS BEYOND OUR CONTROL.

YOU HAVE TRANSMOGRIFIED INTO THE **MOST** POWERFUL OF MAGICAL BEINGS.
A GIANT OTTER.
YES.
THIS IS **FIFTY** KINDS OF AWESOME! A GIANT SUPERNATURAL **OTTER!**
IT'S **OTTER-LY** OUTSTANDING!
YOU GET IT?
OTTERLY, LIKE THE WORD "UTTERLY."
WE GOT IT.
ARE YOU WEARING TIGHTS?
YES. DO YOU WANT SOME?
YES.

BRING ME THE NESTOR!

I'VE GOT GIANT MAGIC **OTTER** JUICE NOW!

WOW.
OTTERS! WHO KNEW?!
AND I THOUGHT THE NEATEST THING OTTERS COULD DO WAS FLOAT ON THEIR BACKS AND EAT FOOD OFF THEIR BELLIES!

THIS IS SO MUCH COOLER!
SO MUCH!
YES. WE SHOULD.

IT IS TIME.

TZOT
TZOT
TZOT
TZOT

PLAP

I COULD GET USED TO THIS.

OH, THAT'S RIGHT--
RUN AWAY!!

CUZ I WAS ABOUT TO GET OTTERLY CRAZY ON YOU.

HA!
YEAH!
UH-OH.

GINA! THE NESTOR ARE GONE.

AW, NO. HE WASN'T RUNNING.

HE WAS CHASING.

STAY WITH DEXTER!

YOU'RE KEEPING ME FROM CHASING MONSTERS!
HEY.
THESE ARE THE NOTES THE NESTOR MADE TO FIND THE GATE.
YOU CAN UNDERSTAND THEM?
I THINK SO.
IF I'M READING THIS RIGHT, WHERE THE GATE TAKES THEM... IS ODD.
I THOUGHT IT'S GOING TO TAKE THEM HOME, RIGHT?
WHERE DOES THE GATE LEAD?
ACTUALLY, IT'S NOT ABOUT WHERE...
IT'S WHEN.

CHAPTER 10

THE GIRL WHO BROKE THE WORLD

MAN. THE NESTOR MUST BE TOO FAR AWAY. I LOST MY OTTER POWER-UP.
SKIIIIIIID

BRIIIIIING

YEAH?!
YOU OKAY?!
SORT OF!
YOU FIND HIM?
I FOUND HIM!

HAVE YOU CAUGHT UP WITH THE NESTOR?!
UH-OH.

TZOT

GINA? YOU OKAY?
AAAAAAAH!

AAAAAA

GINA? ARE YOU OKAY?!

AAAAAH!

AWESOME! YOU'RE AWAKE! C'MON! LET'S CATCH UP WITH GINA!
WHERE'S GINA?

SHE'S CHASING AFTER THAT MAGICAL MONSTER. WE--

DEXTER?!

YOU'RE A **VERY** BAD BABYSITTER!
OH. BOY.
WHAT? WHAT HAPPENED?
NOTHING YET.

BUT I'M **PREEEEETTY** SURE SOMETHING'S **ABOUT** TO HAPPEN.

I SEEK THE NESTOR!

YEAH! I'M HEARING THAT **A LOT** LATELY!

YOU CAN'T HAVE THEM!

I DISAGREE.

GINA! YOU'VE **GOT** TO GET THE NESTOR NOW!

I'M **GOING** TO! BUT I'M NOT THE **ONLY** ONE WHO WANTS THEM!
YOU DON'T UNDERSTAND!

CRUNK

GINA?! GINA?!

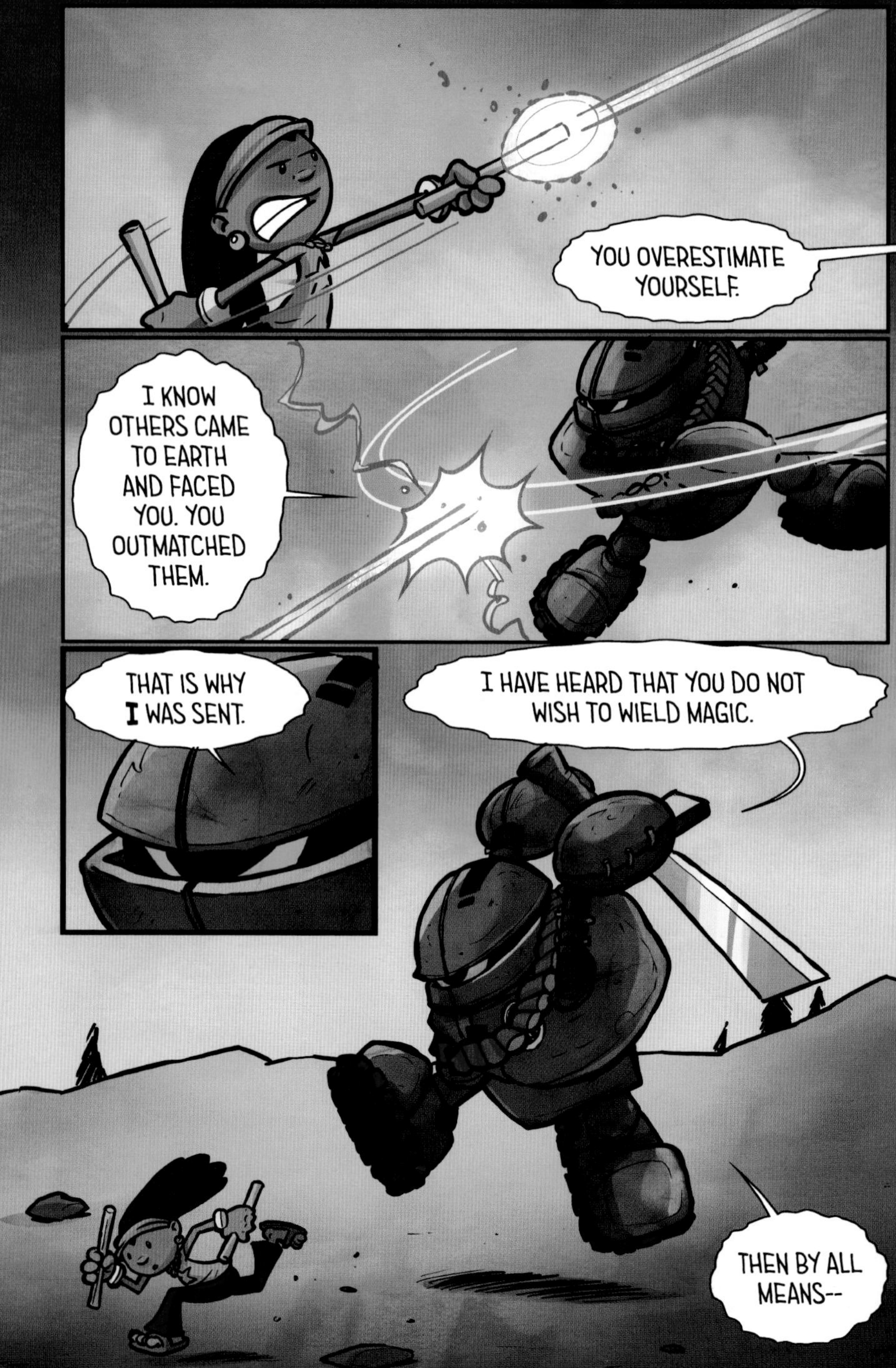
YOU OVERESTIMATE YOURSELF.
I KNOW OTHERS CAME TO EARTH AND FACED YOU. YOU OUTMATCHED THEM.
THAT IS WHY I WAS SENT.
I HAVE HEARD THAT YOU DO NOT WISH TO WIELD MAGIC.
THEN BY ALL MEANS--

GIVE UP.
BOOM

FUMP

YOU ARE MEDDLING WITH FORCES **FAR** BEYOND YOUR UNDERSTANDING.

YOU WILL DO MORE DAMAGE THAN GOOD.

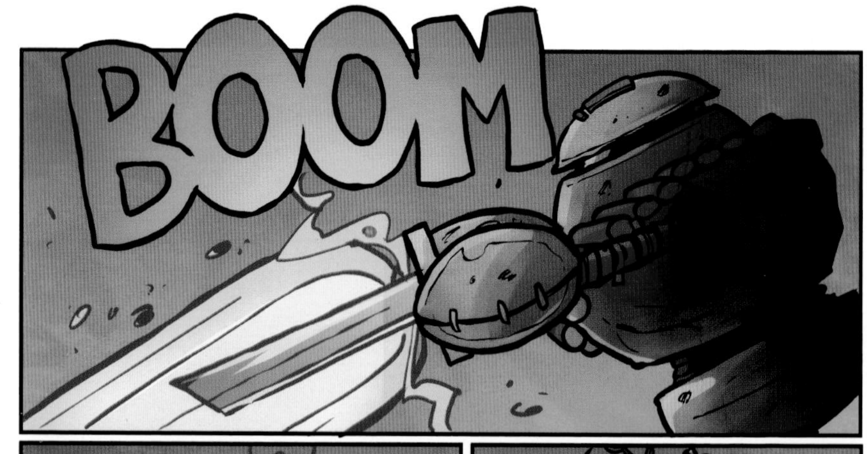
BOOM

CONCENTRATE. IT'S YOUR POWER.

YOU DRAW MAGIC FROM THE **PLANET** ITSELF. YOU **MAKE** MAGIC.

YOU WOULDN'T LET ANYTHING HAPPEN TO US.

WALK AWAY, CHILD.

THIS IS NOT WHO YOU ARE.

YOU BREAK IT, YOU BOUGHT IT.

NO.

I THINK **THIS** IS EXACTLY WHO I AM.

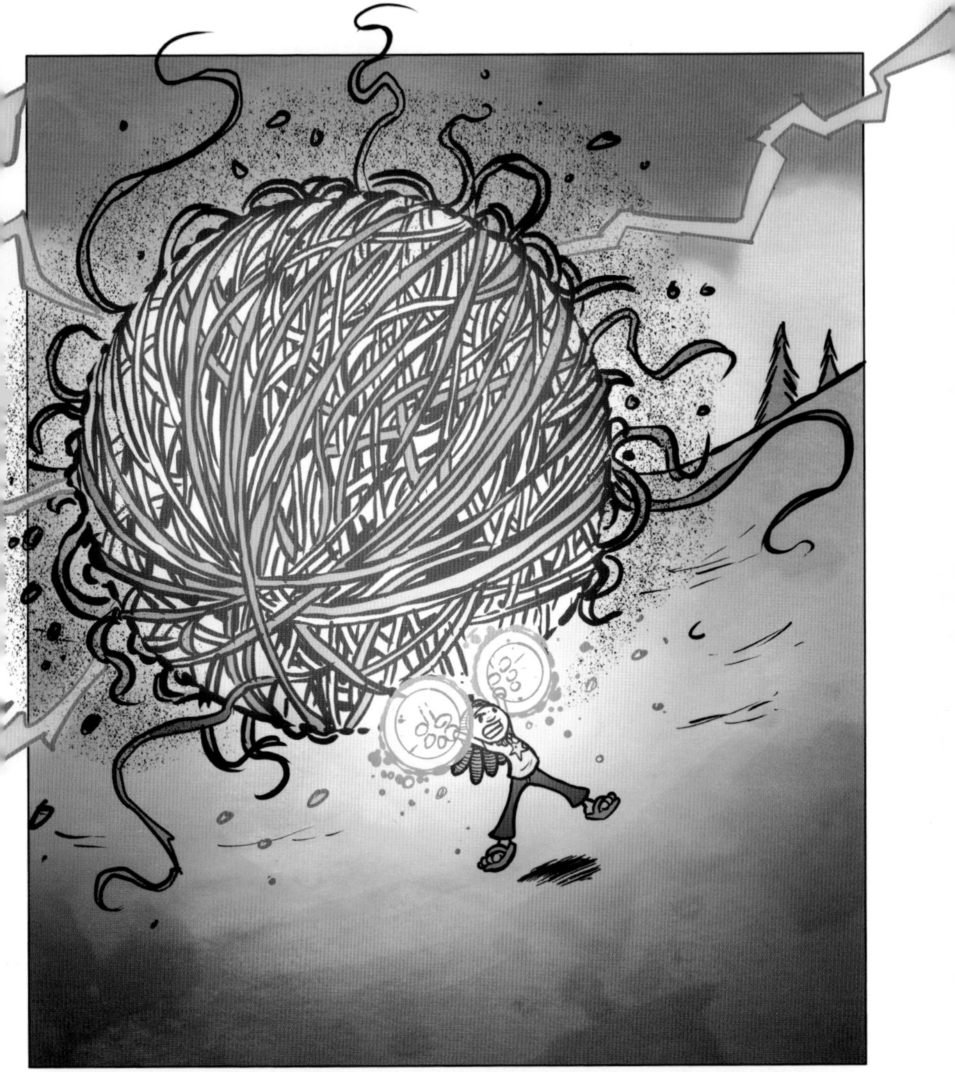

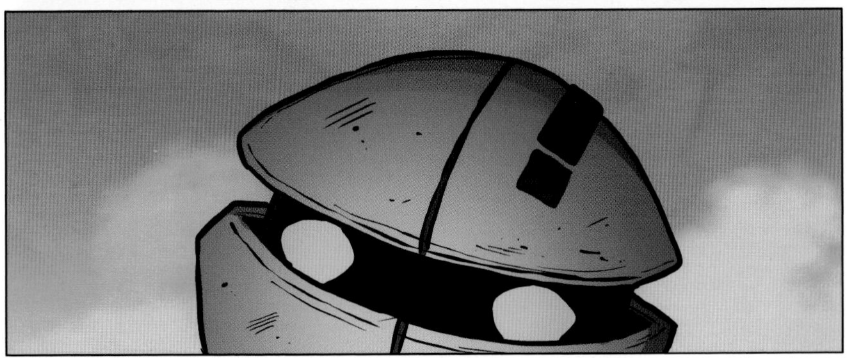

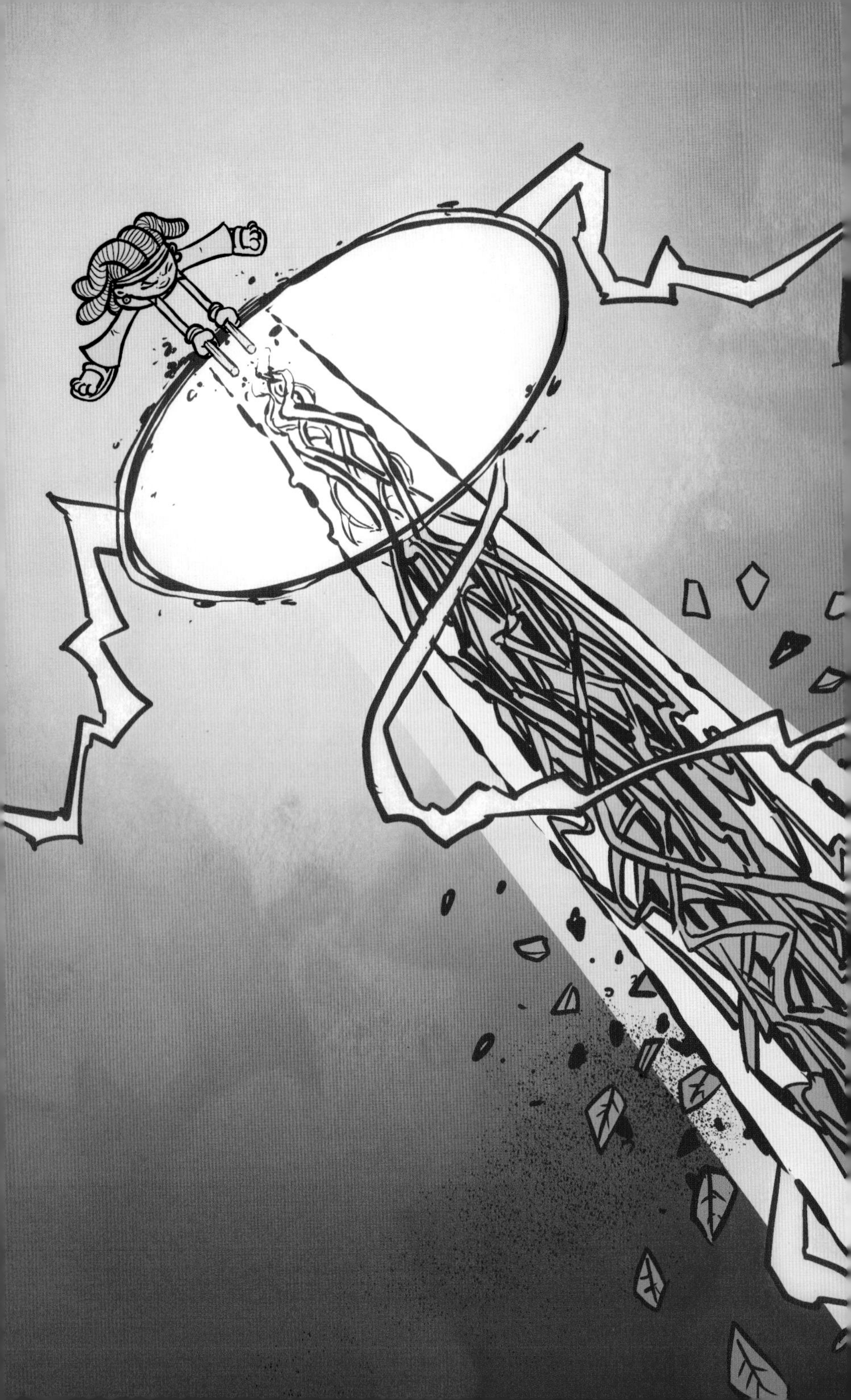

WHY...

WHY...WHY DO THIS?

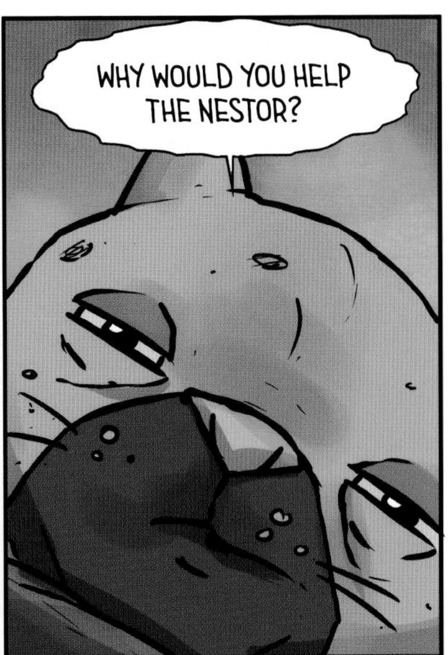
WHY WOULD YOU HELP THE NESTOR?

THEY AREN'T HURTING ANYONE. WHY WOULD **YOU** TRY TO DESTROY THEM?

WE CAME TO HELP YOU.

WE CAME TO PROTECT YOUR WORLD FROM THE NESTOR.

PROTECT OUR WORLD?

YES. **TIME** IS NOT TO BE TAMPERED WITH.

GOOD LUCK TO YOU AND YOUR WORLD, GINA COOPER.

POOF

TIME?

CRUD AND SCRAMBLED EGGS.

...THERE HAS BEEN NO MAGIC ON EARTH IN 100,000 YEARS.

...MAGIC **REMOVED** ITSELF FROM THIS WORLD.

THE NESTOR WERE HERE ON THIS WORLD. IT WAS A SIMPLER TIME FOR ALL.

STOP!!

PLEASE! STOP!!

HELLO, GINA COOPER!

WE ARE **SO** GLAD YOU ARE SAFE!

NO! YOU WANT TO GO BACK IN **TIME!**

THAT IS THE **ONLY** WAY WE CAN GO HOME! BACK TO **BEFORE** WE WERE DISCOVERED! BACK TO BEFORE WE WERE **HUNTED!**

BACK TO WHERE IT ALL BEGAN.

TEEEEEEEEEN

IF YOU GO BACK IN TIME, IT MAY CHANGE THE FUTURE!
PLEASE DON'T DO THIS! LET ME HELP YOU FIND ANOTHER WAY!

THERE **IS** NO OTHER WAY!

NO!

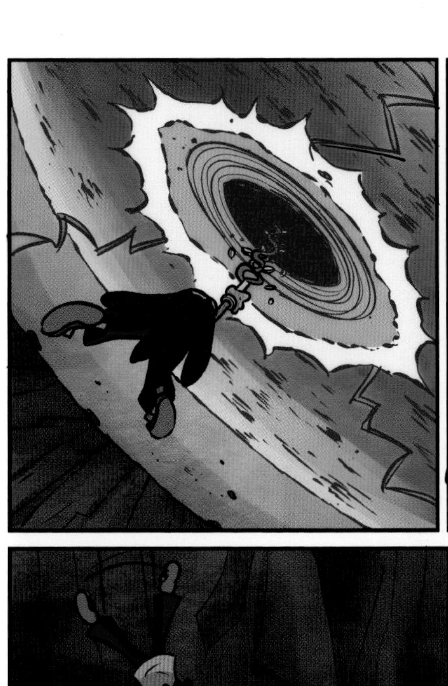

POOF

SPLOOSH

NO.

THEY'RE GOING BACK IN TIME!!

YOU GOTTA... STOP THEM... BEFORE THEY GO BACK.

I WAS TOO LATE.

OH.
BUT EVERYTHING SEEMS OKAY.

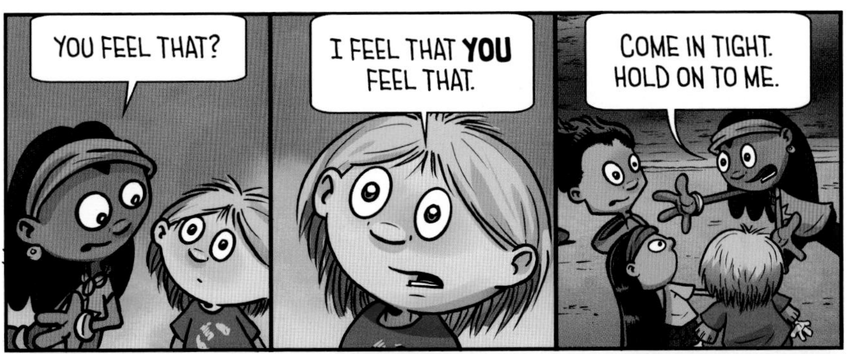
YOU FEEL THAT?
I FEEL THAT **YOU** FEEL THAT.
COME IN TIGHT. HOLD ON TO ME.

WHAT'S HAPPENING?!
I'VE GOT YOU.

I WON'T LET ANYTHING HAPPEN TO YOU.

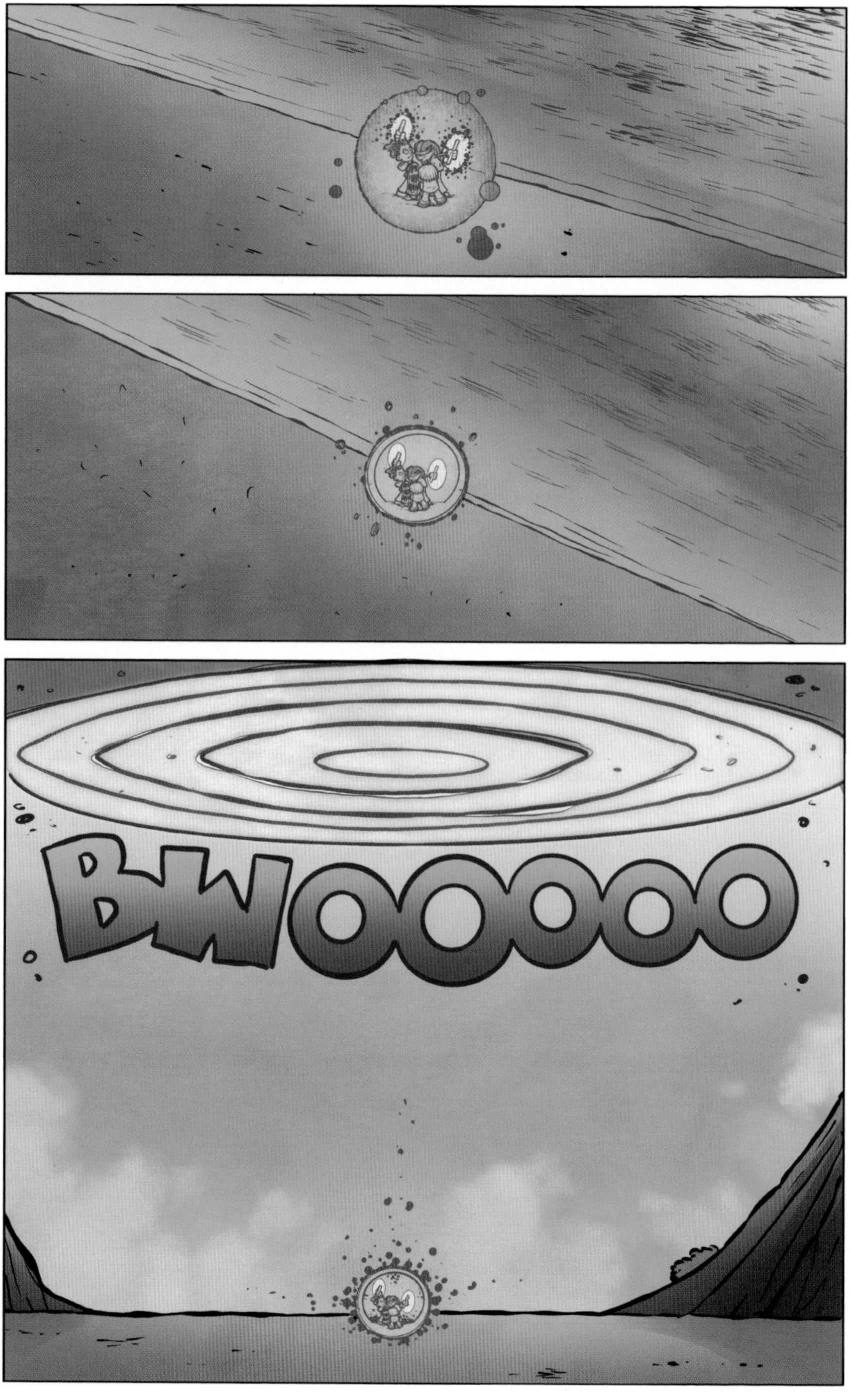

BWOOOOO

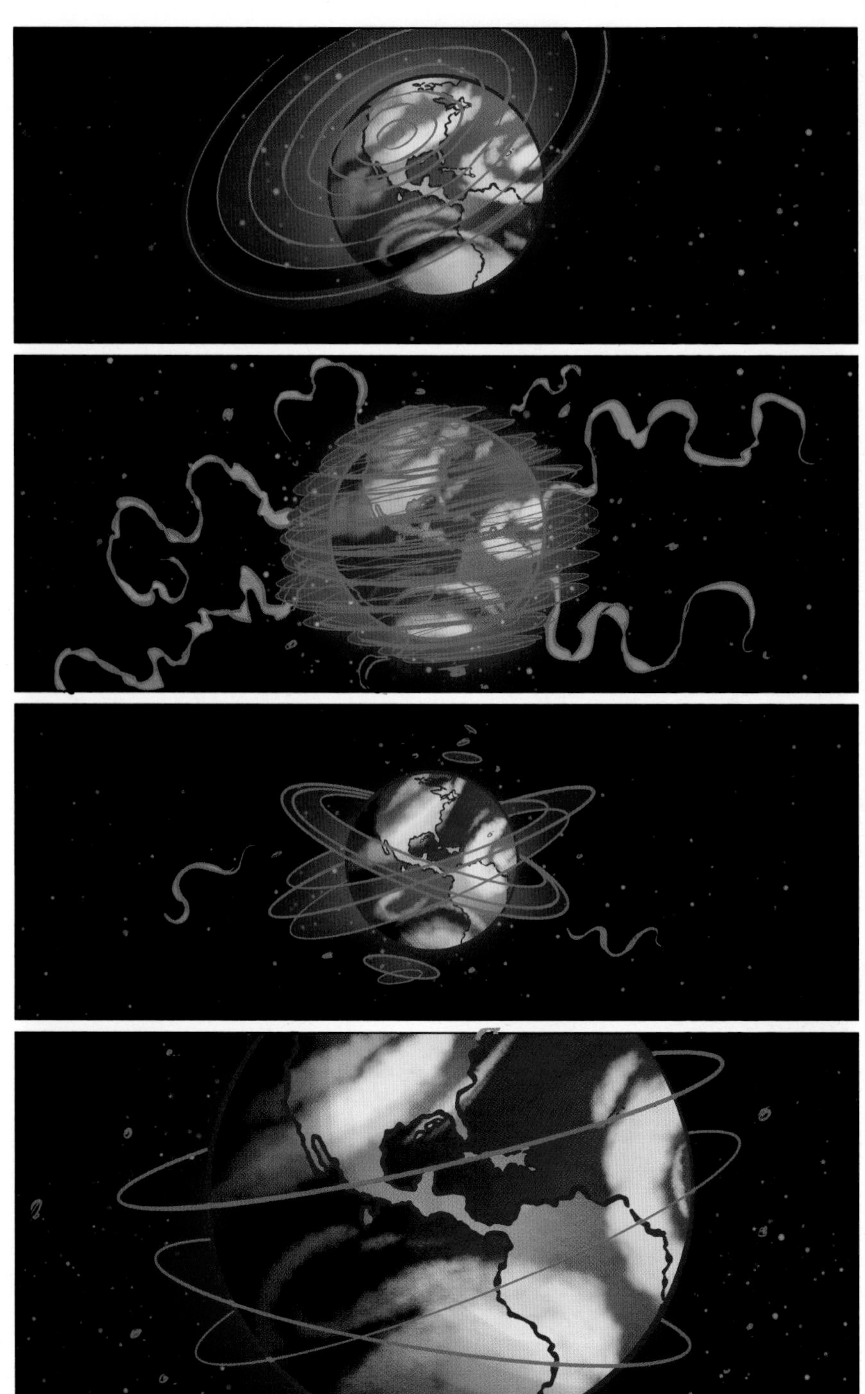

HWEEEEN

WHAT...WHAT HAPPENED?

I CAN...I **FEEL** IT.

THE NESTOR WENT BACK IN TIME. THEY WENT BACK TO THE TIME **BEFORE** MAGIC LEFT EARTH.

THEY **CHANGED** THE EARTH'S HISTORY.
SO NOW... FOR THE LAST 100,000 YEARS...
MAGIC HAS RULED THE EARTH.

EVERYTHING'S CHANGED?

EVERYTHING.
EVERYTHING EXCEPT US.

I SHIELDED US.

WE ARE THE ONLY FOUR PEOPLE ON EARTH WHO REMEMBER WHAT THE EARTH IS REALLY LIKE.

WHAT ARE WE GOING TO DO?

YOU BREAK IT,
YOU BOUGHT IT.

I BROKE THE WORLD.

NOW I HAVE TO FIX IT.

END OF BOOK SEVEN

The adventure continues in...

HILO

BOOK 8

GINA – THE BIG SECRET

Coming in spring 2022!

Read ALL the HILOS!

JUDD WINICK is the creator of the award-winning, **New York Times** bestselling Hilo series. Judd grew up on Long Island with a healthy diet of doodling, **X-Men** comics, the newspaper strip **Bloom County,** and **Looney Tunes.** Today, he lives in San Francisco with his wife, Pam Ling; their two kids; their cat, Chaka; and far too many action figures and vinyl toys for a normal adult. Judd created the Cartoon Network series **Juniper Lee;** has written issues of superhero comics, including Batman, Green Lantern, and Green Arrow; and was a cast member of MTV's **The Real World: San Francisco.** Judd is also the author of the highly acclaimed graphic novel **Pedro and Me,** about his **Real World** roommate and friend, AIDS activist Pedro Zamora. Visit Judd and Hilo online at juddspillowfort.com or find him on Twitter at @JuddWinick.